Natur

Earthquake!

by

Godwin Chu

Don Johnston Incorporated
Volo, Illinois

Edited by:
Jerry Stemach, MS, CCC-SLP
AAC Specialist, Adaptive Technology Center, Sonoma County, California

Gail Portnuff Venable, MS, CCC-SLP
Speech-Language Pathologist, Scottish Rite Center for Childhood Language Disorders, San Francisco, California

Dorothy Tyack, MA
Learning Disabilities Specialist, Scottish Rite Center for Childhood Language Disorders, San Francisco, California

Consultant: Ted S. Hasselbring, PhD
Professor of Special Education, Vanderbilt University, Nashville, TN

Cover Design: Susan Baptist
Interior Illustrations: Jeff Ham and Susan Baptist
Cover Photographs: Roger Ressmeyer/CORBIS and the National Archives
Read by: Denise Jordan-Walker
Sound Engineer: Tom Krol, *TK Audio Studios*

Published by:

Don Johnston Incorporated
26799 West Commerce Drive
Volo, IL 60073
800.999.4660 USA Canada
800.889.5242 Tech Support
www.donjohnston.com

International Standard Book Number
ISBN 1-58702-367-9

Contents

Chapter 1

On Solid Ground

National Archives

I like to think that I am always on solid ground. When I go hiking in the mountains, the ground feels solid. When I sit on the grass in the park, the ground feels solid there, too. But is it really solid? No! At least not when there's an earthquake!

Earthquakes are mysterious things. They are invisible. No one knows when an earthquake will strike or how big it will be. Yet earthquakes happen every day, all over the world.

There have been earthquakes ever since the earth began to take shape. In fact, by the time you finish reading this sentence, there will probably be an earthquake somewhere in the world. Every year, there are 800,000 small quakes called *tremors*. But most of them happen out in the middle of the ocean or they are too small for us to notice.

Over the years, people have observed that animals will often behave strangely right before an earthquake. Dogs bark and scratch at doors.

Cats meow and run around wildly. Birds fly in circles for hours, then suddenly fly away right before the shaking starts. Animals may do these things because they feel the vibrations before we do.

People all over the world have made up myths and stories to try to explain earthquakes.

Long ago, in Russia, people thought that earthquakes were caused by a giant bull that lived underground. When the bull moved, the earth shook.

In Chile, a country in South America, people said that earthquakes were caused by two snakes fighting. One snake dug holes in the earth, and the other snake filled up the holes with stones.

In China, people believed that the earth was held up in the sky by a large dragon. When the dragon shook its head, there would be earthquakes.

In India, people believed that earthquakes were caused by a giant elephant walking across the land.

The Indians of North America believed that the earth rested on the back of a giant turtle, and that earthquakes happened whenever the turtle took a step.

These are stories that people have made up to try to make sense of something that they didn't understand. It would be a long time before scientists learned what really causes earthquakes.

Chapter 2

San Francisco, 1906

It was early in the morning in San Francisco on Wednesday, April 18, 1906. The sun was just coming up in the sky, but already the air was warm. The city had been very hot for two days. This was strange for San Francisco, which is usually cool in the spring. Some people called it "earthquake weather." But most people thought this was silly. "Hot weather doesn't bring earthquakes," they said. Then, at 5:13 in the morning, the ground began to shake.

Andy Cooper and his wife, Sarah, were asleep when the earthquake struck. Their bedroom was on the second floor. The shaking started slowly. They heard a low rumble, and things began to rattle all over the house. Then the shaking became violent. The rumbling and rattling turned into a roar. A picture fell off the wall and hit Andy on the head. It sounded as if a train was rolling through their room.

"It's an earthquake!" Andy said to his wife.

They both jumped out of bed. Sarah ran to the next room to grab their baby daughter. Andy stood in the doorway of the bedroom, and Sarah stood in the doorway across the hall holding the baby. All around them, furniture fell over. The house creaked and groaned. Andy was sure that the wooden walls of the house would snap in two.

The brick chimney toppled over and fell through the roof. It crashed through the ceiling and floor of the bedroom and landed in the living room. A large telephone pole fell through the window. Sarah screamed, and the baby began to cry.

The shaking lasted for almost a full minute. Then everything was quiet again.

Andy and Sarah carefully made their way out of the house. Many of their neighbors were already standing outside in their pajamas.

Some had not even had time to put on their shoes. Andy looked up and down the street. Telephone poles and street signs were bent over at crazy angles. Some of the buildings were leaning at dangerous angles, too.

The sidewalks were covered with bricks and glass. Many trees had fallen into the street. There were hundreds of cracks in the sidewalk. People just looked at each other. They did not know what to do next.

National Archives

Then the ground shook again. It was a smaller quake than the first one, but it was strong enough to make some of the damaged houses fall down completely. Andy moaned as he watched his own house collapse. There would be many more small earthquakes, called *aftershocks*, in the days to come. People held onto each other. They were afraid to go back into their homes.

Chapter 3

The Great Fire Starts

Next came the dogs. Dozens of dogs made their way slowly up the hill where Andy and Sarah's house was. The dogs were whimpering. They were breathing hard and their tongues were hanging out. They had been running for a long time. They looked tired and scared. Many of the dogs just lay down in the middle of the street when they reached the top of the hill. People were amazed. Why had all these dogs run up the hill?

Andy looked down the hill at the city below. Now he could see why the dogs had been running. Andy could see at least ten pillars of black smoke curling up into the sky. Small fires were burning all over San Francisco!

The south side of the city was on fire. The small fires grew larger and joined together into several huge fires. They were spreading across the city. Andy knew that the fires would soon follow the dogs up the hills.

Suddenly, a house at the end of Andy's street caught fire. A gas line had broken in the quake. Then somebody had tossed a cigarette near the broken pipe and this had started the fire. The fire spread to the house next door. Soon all the buildings on the street would be burning.

Now people *did* run inside their houses. They grabbed as many of their things as they could carry and piled them outside in the street.

Andy crawled into his crumbled house and put some photos, letters, jewelry, and money into a wooden chest. Two men helped him pull the chest out into the street. Then Andy went back inside and got some clothes for Sarah and the baby and for himself.

One family on Andy's block owned a car, but the car had been destroyed in the quake. So all of the families on the block had to push and pull and carry their things down the street.

"We won't get very far pushing this wooden chest down the street," Sarah said. "We need to bury it in the ground so that it won't be burned."

Andy ran into the nearest garage and found a shovel. The fire was now only a few houses away. He dug a large hole in the ground. Then he dumped the chest into the hole and covered it with dirt.

"How will I remember this spot?" he asked himself. He saw that there was a fire hydrant right across the sidewalk from his hole.

The hydrant was broken and not a single drop of water came through the pipe.

"That hydrant won't help us put out this fire," he thought to himself. "But at least it will help me find our chest later."

Andy gave the clothes to Sarah. Then he took the baby and they started to run down the street. Sarah looked back over her shoulder just in time to see their house burst into flames.

Chapter 4

Dynamite

Andy's brother, John, had been hitchhiking to San Francisco for a visit when the earthquake struck. John's last ride was on a wagon that was pulled by two horses. The wagon was piled high with boxes.

"What's in all of those boxes?" John asked the driver.

"Dynamite," replied the man. "Those fires in San Francisco are out of control. The quake broke the water lines," he said.

"There are too many fires and not enough water to put them out. There are not enough firemen either," the man explained. "We're going to blow up the buildings that are in the path of the fire. When the fire has no more buildings to burn, it will die out and the rest of the city will be saved," he said.

When the wagon reached the city, it seemed as if everything was on fire. The smoke was so thick that the sun looked blood red. The smoke in the sky turned red and yellow and brown.

All along Market Street, there were cars and wagons carrying dead or wounded people. The drivers had to steer around the twisted steel tracks that had once been used by the streetcar.

The wagon full of dynamite turned down Van Ness Avenue. There was destruction everywhere. Buildings were lying on their sides. Some looked as if parts had been cut off with a giant ax.

Then John saw what was left of City Hall. Its stone pillars were in pieces on the ground. All that remained standing was the steel frame of its great dome.

The fire was spreading fast. The heat of the fire pulled the air in from all sides. An eerie wind blew into the center of the fire, and flames shot up into the sky. The buildings fed the fire, and the wind kept the flames burning. The firemen had decided to blow up the homes on Van Ness Avenue because it was one of the widest streets in the city.

National Archives

The firemen were hoping that the fire would burn itself out there.

John helped the firemen to unload the dynamite. Then he went to look for Andy and Sarah and their baby. People were pushing heavy carts down the street and carrying bags and suitcases in their arms. When they got too tired, they just left their clothes and furniture in big piles on the street.

There were many dead bodies lying on the ground. Some of the people had died in the quake, and others had been burned in the fire. In front of a broken store window, John saw a dead man with a sign on top of him that said, "Looter." The things that the man had stolen from the store were lying next to his body. John stopped to read a sign on the wall of the store. The sign had a message from the mayor of San Francisco.

To the People of
San Francisco
LOOTER

TO THE PEOPLE OF SAN FRANCISCO

I have ordered the army and police to KILL anybody caught stealing or committing any other crime. Several men have already been shot to death for looting.

We will not turn the gas and electricity back on until it is safe, so the city will be without power until that time.

Everybody should stay at home between dusk and dawn until order is restored. Because of the danger from broken gas pipes, do not light any matches.

If we all help each other during this emergency, we will survive.

—E. E. Schmitz, Mayor

April 18, 1906

When John got to Andy and Sarah's house, he found that all of the houses on their street had been burned to the ground. All that remained were piles of bricks, broken stones, bent pipes and black ash.

It was the same all over the city. "San Francisco is in ruins," John thought to himself. He prayed that Andy and Sarah and the baby were still alive. He wondered if he would ever see them again.

Chapter 5

The Days After the Quake

The days after the quake were full of confusion. Thousands of people had no homes so they were taken across the bay to Oakland by boat. In Oakland, there were more places for people to stay. Thousands more people were taken away by train to other safe areas.

More than half of all the people living in San Francisco were forced to move.

The people who stayed in the city went into Golden Gate Park and out to Ocean Beach to get away from the fire. John followed a long line of people up Fell Street to the park.

The park was crowded with people. The army was in charge of helping them. The soldiers made sure that everyone had a tent and enough water and food. John got into a long line. When he reached the front of the line, a soldier gave him a blanket and a tent.

That night, John was lying inside his tent when he heard a child's voice.

"I want to go home, Mama," a little girl said. "I want to go home to my bed."

"We haven't any home, dear," the girl's mother answered. "Now lie down under this tree," she said in a soft voice.

John stepped out of his tent and offered to trade places with the woman and child.

The woman smiled at him and said, "Thank you, sir. That's very kind of you." And she went inside the tent with her little girl.

John lay down under the tree, but he could not fall asleep. There were no lights in the park, but the fires were burning so brightly that he could see well enough to write in his diary.

He sat up and wrote:

> There are hundreds of people here with me in the park. I guess that the quake and fire have destroyed almost everything they owned. Now, rich people have no more than poor people. Perhaps this is good. A human life is the only thing that's really worth anything. Tomorrow I will look again for my brother and his wife and child.

In the morning, John was awakened by a voice yelling, "Cooks needed! Can you cook?"

John went to help make breakfast. Then he stood at a table and handed out bread to each person in line.

John was cutting a loaf of bread when he heard a voice say, “I hope you saved a piece of bread for me, brother.” John looked up and saw his brother, Andy, standing in front of him with Sarah and the baby.

“As a matter of fact, I have been saving this loaf just for you,” John answered, throwing his arms around them.

Sarah stepped up. She was holding the baby. She gave John a big hug.

The city would never be the same again. More than 3,000 people had died. Many of their names will never be known. San Francisco would have to be completely rebuilt.

But on that morning, John looked around at all of the people and he felt happy. He had found his family, and he was ready to help them start over. No earthquake was going to shake them apart.

Chapter 6

Who Invented the Richter Scale?

Bettman/CORBIS

When the earth moves in a quake, the shaking releases energy. In 1935, a scientist named Charles Richter invented a way to measure how much the ground moved in a quake and the amount of energy that was released by the shaking. He did this by using a tool called a *seismograph*.

The first part of the word, "seismo," comes from the word *seismic*. Seismo is a word that means earthquakes. The second part of the word, "graph," means something that is written down.

The word *seismograph* means "picture of an earthquake."

The seismograph gives us information about the shaking motions in the ground.

The Richter Scale shows us how much energy is released by an earthquake. The Richter Scale uses the information from the seismograph to calculate the strength, or *magnitude*, of the quake.

An earthquake can be felt for many miles. But the quake is strongest at the place where it starts. Scientists call that place the *epicenter*.

What is the difference between an earthquake that is 5.3 on the Richter Scale and one that is 8.3? What do the numbers mean?

The Richter Scale goes from 1 to 9. We can hardly feel an earthquake of "1." Scientists think that an earthquake of "9" is the strongest quake that can ever happen.

Roger Ressmeyer/CORBIS

But the jump from one number to the next is no small thing.

Every time the Richter Scale goes up one point, it means that the quake is ten times stronger. For example, the difference between 5.0 and 8.0 is 3. This means that the 8.0 quake is 10 x 10 x 10 times stronger than the 5.0 quake. 10 x 10 x 10 = 1,000, so the 8.0 quake is 1,000 times more powerful than the 5.0 quake!

A 5.0 quake would be a medium-sized quake. Scientists guess that the quake that hit San Francisco in 1906 was an 8.3 quake. It was one of the strongest earthquakes ever in California.

Chapter 7

The Layers of Earth

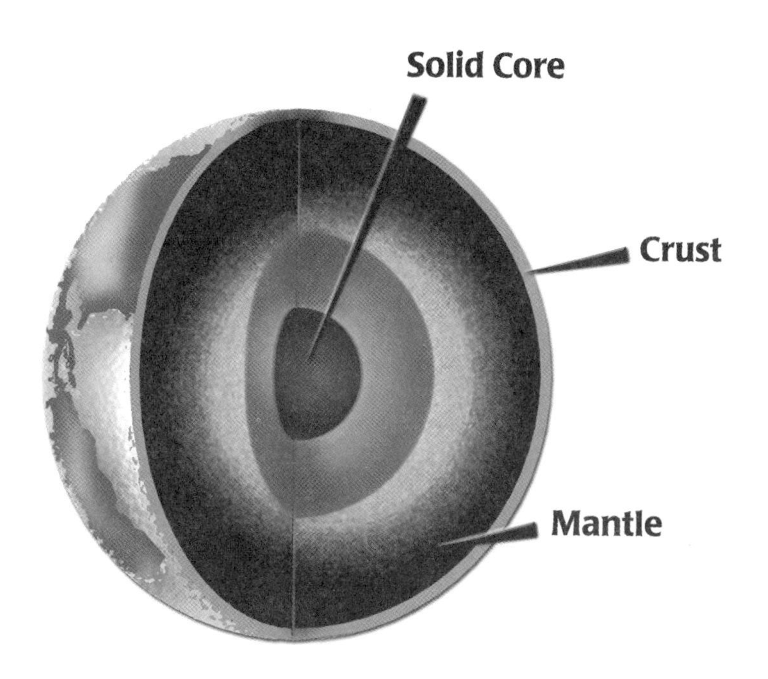

We all live on the surface of the earth. Earthquakes begin deep inside the earth and travel through miles of rock before reaching the surface where we are.

We know that the earth is made up of three main layers. At the center of the earth is the *core*. The core is made up of solid metals like iron and nickel.

The next layer is called the *mantle*. The mantle is made up of hot melted rock that is always moving. This melted rock is called *magma*.

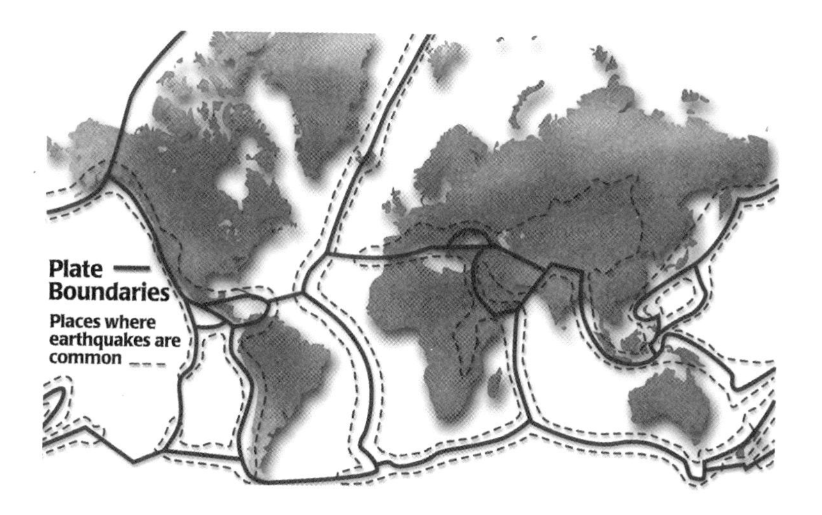
Plate Boundaries
Places where earthquakes are common

The very top layer of the earth is called the *crust*. This is where we live. The crust is made up of different types of rock and it is between 3 and 25 miles thick.

At first, scientists believed that the crust of the earth was all one piece. But now we know that the crust is actually broken up into 12 large pieces called *tectonic plates*. Some of these plates are very large. In fact, most of North America rests on just one plate. The bottom of the whole Pacific Ocean rests on a different plate!

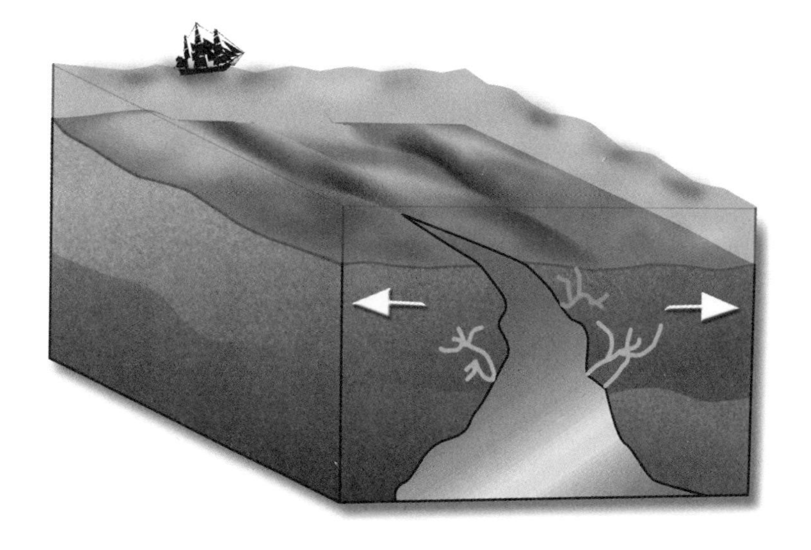

So the earth's crust is broken up into plates, and these plates are always moving. They move very slowly. Some plates slide against each other, some bump into each other, and some slide under other plates.

As the plates move, the land above them moves, also. Scientists say that the land *drifts*. This is how the continents were formed. We call this movement *continental drift*.

But what causes the plates to move? Remember that there is melted rock, or magma, in the mantle underneath the plates. It is the melted rock that makes the plates move.

If you drop a few grains of rice into a pot of boiling water, you will see that the boiling water moves the rice around in a circle. First, the grains of rice move up the sides of the pot, then back down the center of the pot, and then back up the sides again.

This kind of motion is called *convection*. Convection also happens to the melted rock in the mantle of the earth.

If you toss a few crackers on top of the boiling water, you will see that the crackers float around the top of the water, bumping into each other. This is caused by the convection of the boiling water under the crackers.

In the same way, the movement of the plates is caused by the magma in the hot mantle.

The movement of the plates is called *plate tectonics* and plate tectonics is what causes earthquakes.

Most earthquakes happen in the places where the plates touch each other. The places where plates come together are called *faults*. There are three different types of faults.

In the first kind of fault, two plates collide and grind against each other. This pushing of the two plates builds up a lot of energy, or *stress*. Finally, this causes an earthquake. This is also how mountains are made.

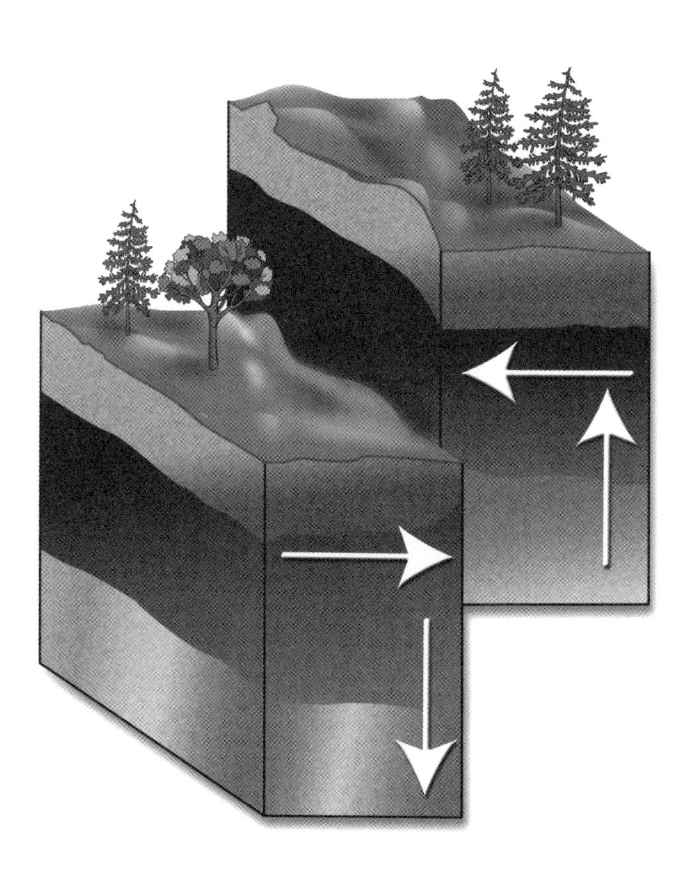

Millions of years ago, earthquakes caused the Himalayan mountains of Asia to rise up. One of these mountains, Mount Everest, is the tallest mountain in the world. Mount Everest is over 29,000 feet tall.

In the second type of fault, two plates slide past one another. This sliding causes a lot of earthquakes, because the plates are uneven and the rocks are bumpy. The San Andreas Fault in California is this kind of fault.

The city of Los Angeles sits on a plate that is moving northward. As it moves, it scrapes up against the other plate, causing earthquakes. These plates move or drift very slowly, at about two inches per year. In fact, in billions of years, Los Angeles may end up farther north than San Francisco!

In the third type of fault, one plate slides underneath another plate. This is called *subduction*. As one plate slides underneath the other, the tip of the bottom plate is forced downward.

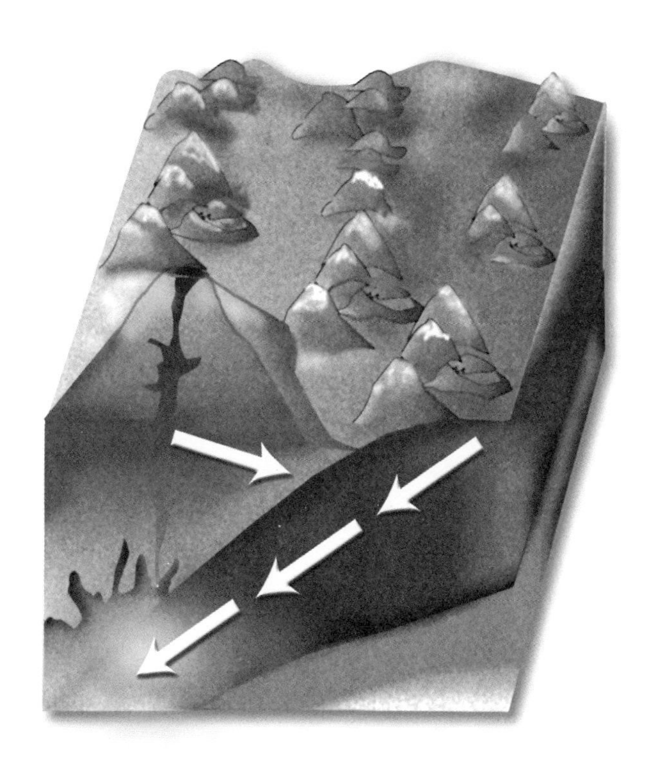

As the tip of the bottom plate gets down to 50 miles below the surface, it melts. Two things can happen. First, as one plate slides under the other, there may be an earthquake. Second, the melted rock can erupt out of the earth and become lava. That is how volcanoes are born. That's why there are usually earthquakes before a volcano erupts.

Chapter 8

An Earthquake in Missouri

The most active areas in the world for earthquakes lie all around the shores of the Pacific Ocean. These areas make up the Pacific Rim. The Pacific Rim includes Japan, Southeast Asia, the east coast of Australia, the west coasts of South America and North America, and Alaska. Most of the world's active volcanoes are also found in the Pacific Rim. In fact, the Pacific Rim is also known as the "Ring of Fire."

Earthquakes don't always happen in places where the ocean meets the land. One of the largest earthquakes ever recorded in North America happened right in the center of the country. It was in New Madrid, Missouri, on December 16, 1811.

On that day, the people in New Madrid felt a sudden jolt. Then they heard the ground start to rumble.

The rumble slowly became a roar. Then the ground began to shake, and the trees groaned as if they might break.

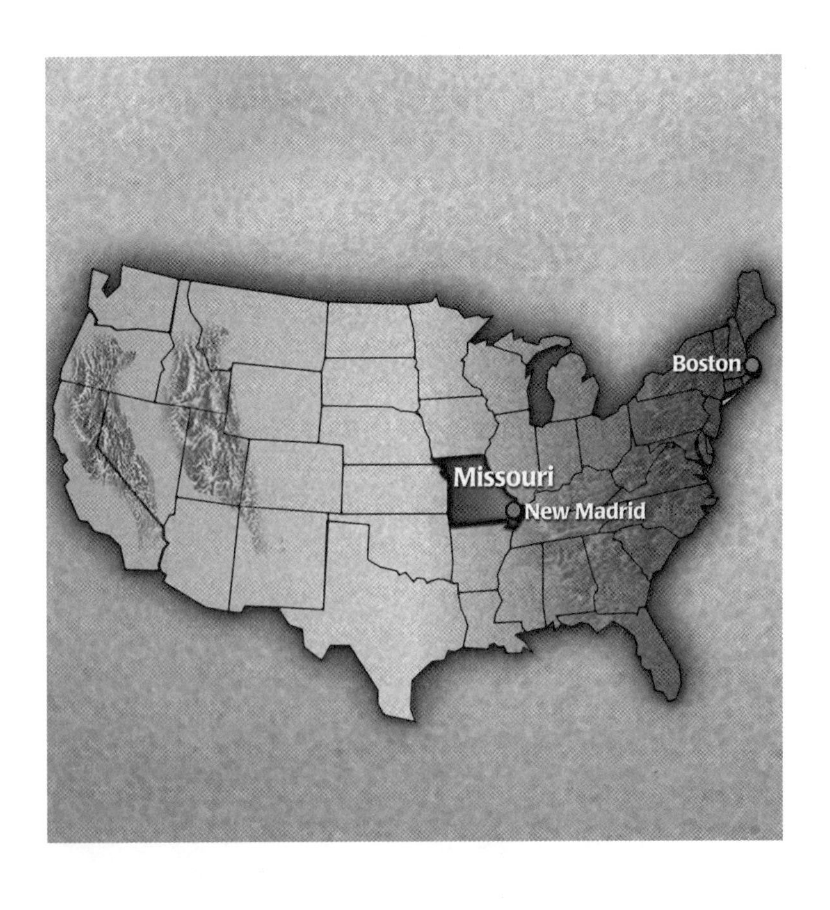
Boston
Missouri
New Madrid

Holes appeared in the ground, and water shot out of these holes and up into the air. The river began to move faster and faster, and water crashed onto the shore. A sandy island in the middle of the river suddenly sank. Hills started to crumble. A huge hole opened in the ground, swallowed up some cows, and then closed back up again.

Everything was quiet for a while. Then the earthquakes started again. The quakes went on like that for the next month.

The quakes were so strong that they changed the path of the Mississippi River. Church bells in Boston, Massachusetts started to ring all by themselves, even though Boston is 1,000 miles away from Missouri.

Why did this earthquake happen in New Madrid? Nobody knows for sure. But scientists believe that the quakes were caused by cracks deep within the North American plate.

The North American plate is about 3,000 miles across and about 25 miles thick. That's a very big and heavy rock, and it's cracked! Just think about it – the entire continent is sitting on top of a cracked rock! After millions of years, the pressure becomes too much, and the rock needs to shift slightly in order to keep holding up all that weight. It's a little like having a chair with a weak leg. People may sit in the chair for many days with no problems, but one day the chair will suddenly break.

Chapter 9

Tsunami!

What happens when an earthquake occurs below the ocean floor? Most of the time, quakes out in the ocean do not have any effect on people. That's because there's usually nobody around! But sometimes quakes below the ocean can have an effect on people living far away from where the quake actually took place.

Have you ever thrown a rock into a pond? First, there is a "plop" as the rock hits the water and sinks.

And then, from the spot where the rock hit the water, you can see ripples slowly spreading out until they reach the shore of the pond.

This is also what happens when there is an earthquake below the ocean. The quake acts just like a giant rock that is thrown into the water. The quake makes a series of *shock waves* that move through the water.

But, instead of little ripples on a pond, these shock waves spread out across the ocean until they reach a beach that may be hundreds of miles away.

The waves start out small. If you were on a ship out at sea, you would probably not even notice these waves passing under your boat. But the waves become very large. They can be up to 60 miles long and hundreds of miles wide, and they can also move as fast as 375 miles an hour. When the waves get that big and that fast, watch out!

The ocean becomes more shallow near land. When this big wave gets close to shore, it starts to slow down.

But the wave also grows bigger and taller as it gets closer to the shore because there is so much water moving up fast from behind. When a wave like this hits land, it can be over 80 feet high. It can cause a lot of damage and kill many people.

Some people call this a *tidal wave*. The Japanese call these giant killer waves *tsunami*. “Tsu” is the Japanese word for a village by the seashore and “nami” is the Japanese word for a wave. No one in the village is safe when a tsunami hits the seashore!

In 1896, in Japan, a young girl named Mariko survived a tsunami that crashed over her seaside village.

It was a bright sunny morning, and Mariko was playing with her father on the beach. Suddenly, fish started to jump out of the water onto the sand. One after another, hundreds of fish threw themselves onto the beach and flopped around on the sand. Mariko looked at her father. What was happening?

What were the fish trying to get away from? Then her father remembered that animals sometimes behaved in strange ways when there was an earthquake. He guessed that there must have been a quake somewhere out at sea.

"We must get away from the beach, Mariko," her father said. "A tsunami may be coming. We have to get to higher ground."

Mariko and her father ran for two miles up into the hills behind their village. From there, they watched as a tsunami wave grew out at sea. The wave must have been over 60 feet high when it hit land. The wave swept away the entire village, all of the trees in the fields, and all of the boats in the harbor. There were only a few people who survived. They were the ones who were up in the hills when the tsunami struck.

Chapter 10

Holding Back the Water

Earthquakes are one of the most powerful forces in nature. A large earthquake can be felt hundreds of miles away from where it happens. Sometimes, when an earthquake strikes, even mountains start to crumble.

That is what happened one terrible day in 1970 in Peru. Peru is a country in South America. Most of the towns in Peru sit in valleys between the Andes mountains.

One of these mountains is called Huascaran. Far below this mountain is the town of Yungay.

One day, an earthquake struck in the Andes near Huascaran. The quake caused huge chunks of ice and rocks to roll down from high up on the mountain. This was the start of a *landslide*. As the chunks of rocks and ice came down the mountain, they picked up more rocks and dirt and carried them along. The ice began to melt. The rushing water got mixed with the dirt and turned into mud.

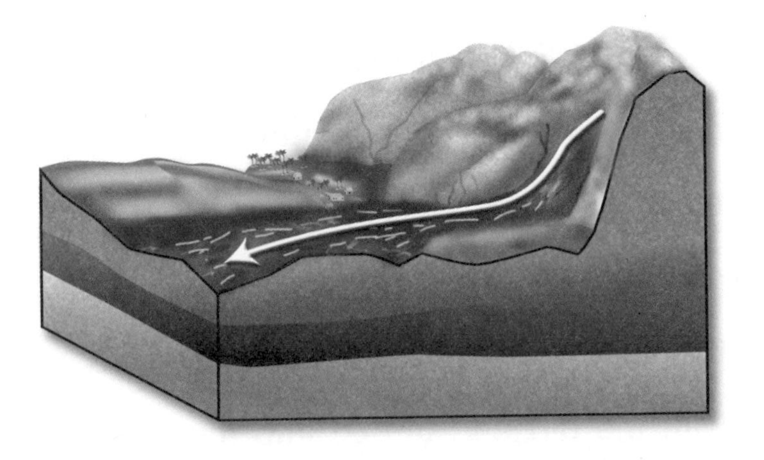

Now the landslide was a *mudflow*. The flow of mud grew bigger and faster as it moved down the side of the mountain. Within a few minutes, it was moving at more than 250 miles an hour.

Far below in the town of Yungay, people heard a deep rumbling sound as the mudflow came closer. A few people saw what was happening and ran for the hills.

The mudflow was like a giant wall of rocks, dirt, and water falling from the sky.

In just three minutes, the mudflow crashed into the valley and destroyed the entire town of Yungay. Only one building was left standing. Almost everyone in the town was killed.

The largest landslide in history happened in China. The Tangshan region in the middle of China is covered with low hills that are made out of loose soil. This type of soil is good for farming, but it also breaks apart very easily.

In 1556, an earthquake in the Tangshan region broke the hills apart. The soil from the hills slid down into the valleys below. This landslide killed more than 830,000 people. It was the largest known earthquake disaster in the history of the world.

As you know, most earthquakes are caused by natural forces in the earth, but sometimes people cause earthquakes, too.

In the late 1930's, the Hoover Dam was built. The Hoover Dam is one of the largest and tallest dams in the world. It was built to hold back the waters of the Colorado River. This would bring water to the farms and towns of Nevada and Arizona. The water behind the dam became Lake Mead. The Hoover Dam made it possible for people to live in the desert because they would always have plenty of water from the lake.

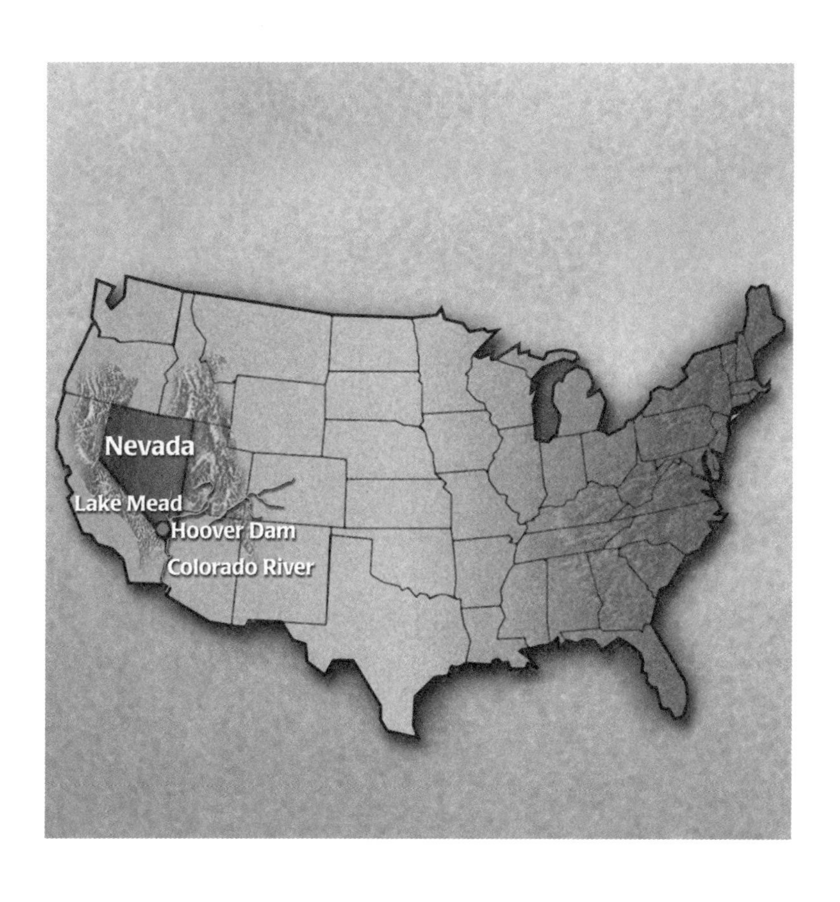
Nevada
Lake Mead
Hoover Dam
Colorado River

But as the dam began to fill up with water, people noticed something strange. As the water got higher behind the dam, the earth started to shake. The quakes started happening more often and they became more violent day by day. Lake Mead was almost full when the largest quake struck. It measured 5.0 on the Richter Scale and it almost caused the dam to crack. It was lucky for everyone that the dam did not break.

National Archives

A dam *did* break in India. In 1967, as the lake behind the Koyna Dam was filling up with water, an earthquake struck. The quake measured 6.3 on the Richter Scale. 200 people were killed and 1,500 more people were injured. Thousands of people were left homeless.

Why did these earthquakes happen? Scientists found out that water behind the dam added new weight to the ground. Water weighs about eight pounds per gallon.

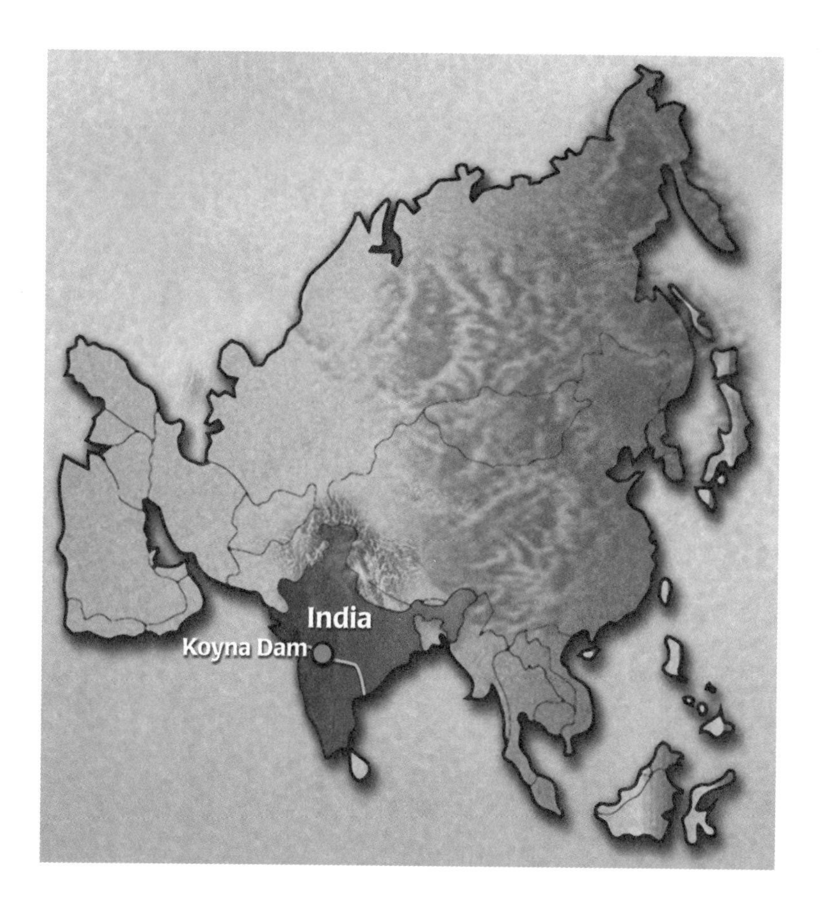
India
Koyna Dam

Millions of gallons of water that used to flow down the river were now being held back by the dam. The lake behind the dam was now much heavier than the river below the dam. The quake was the earth's way of adjusting itself to this shift in weight.

Chapter 11

The Next "Big One"

CORBIS

Nobody knows exactly when or where the next big earthquake will strike. That's because things in the earth can take a long time to change. A thousand years may seem like a long time to you. But for rocks, a thousand years or more is nothing. Remember the earthquakes that took place in Asia millions of years ago? Remember how those earthquakes caused the Himalayan mountains to rise up? Well, earthquakes are still happening there, and those mountains are still getting taller!

AFP/CORBIS

We know that earthquakes can happen anywhere, and at any time. But if you live near the Pacific Rim, the danger of earthquakes is much greater. This means that in the United States, the West Coast is the most dangerous area for earthquakes.

In August 1999, in the country of Turkey, an earthquake that measured 6.8 killed more than 1,200 people and injured thousands more. In 1987, a similar earthquake in Japan killed only two people and injured about 50 people.

Michael S. Yamashita/CORBIS

Why did the quake in Turkey kill so many more people? It was because Japan was better prepared for an earthquake.

The most important thing people can do to prepare for an earthquake is to make sure that their buildings can survive the next quake.

Buildings should stand on solid ground. If you put a brick on top of a bucket of wet sand, and then you shake the bucket, the brick will slowly sink into the sand. This is called *liquefaction*.

Many buildings that are on soft, sandy ground will sink during an earthquake because of liquefaction.

We think of good buildings as being strong and rigid. But if a building is going to survive an earthquake, it needs to be *flexible*. That means that it has to be able to bend without breaking. A building that is made out of brick or stone or mud can't bend.

If you want to build a building that will survive a quake, the best thing to do is to connect the walls and floors to a steel frame.

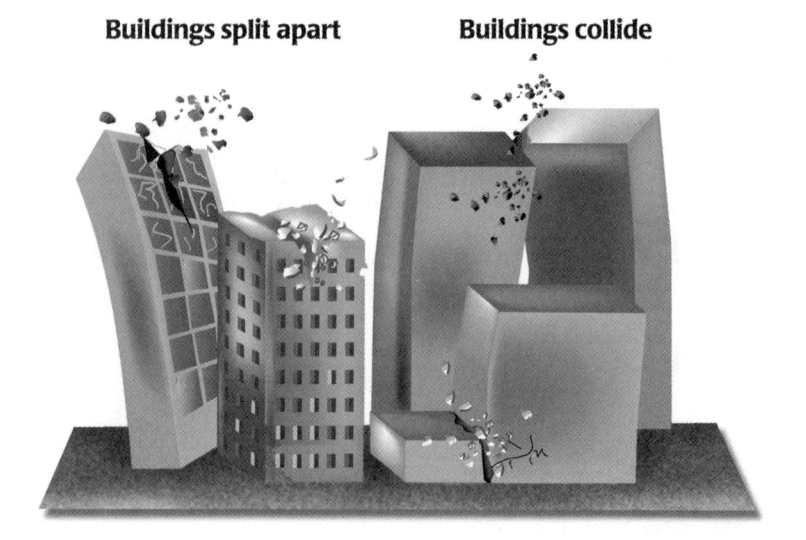
Buildings split apart
Buildings collide

Remember how the dome of San Francisco's City Hall was the only part of the building left standing after the 1906 earthquake? The dome had a steel frame.

A building that is too rigid will fall down in an earthquake. That is what happened in Turkey. But a building that bends *too* much can crash into other buildings or snap into pieces during a quake. The best kind of building is one that can move a little bit with the shock waves of an earthquake.

In Japan, skyscrapers sway during a quake, but they don't break or crack.

If you are in a building during an earthquake, don't run outside! You might get hit by falling objects. You should also stay away from windows, because the glass can break during a quake.

The best thing to do is to stay under a strong table or desk, or stand in a doorway. The frame around a doorway is one of the strongest parts of a building.

The floor, walls, and ceiling will all break before the doorframe.

Earthquakes are part of nature. They happen all the time. Sometimes they cause a lot of damage. But without earthquakes, we would not have any mountains, cliffs, or valleys. Without earthquakes, the different continents would still be locked together as one giant land mass. And without earthquakes, we might have a harder time finding oil and natural gas underground.

That's because the shifting rocks trap pools of oil and natural gas underground.

In the past 50 years, people have learned a lot about how the earth works and why earthquakes happen. People have even caused earthquakes to happen by accident. But we will never be able to prevent earthquakes. The best we can do is be prepared for the next Big One.

The End

A Note from the Start-to-Finish Editors

You will notice that Start-to-Finish Books look different from other high-low readers and chapter books. The text layout of this book coordinates with the other media components (CD and audiocassette) of the Start-to-Finish series.

The text in the book matches, line-for-line and page-for-page, the text shown on the computer screen, enabling readers to follow along easily in the book. Each page ends in a complete sentence so that the student can either practice the page (repeat reading) or turn the page to continue with the story. If the next sentence cannot fit on the page in its entirety, it has been shifted to the next page. For this reason, the sentence at the top of a page may not be indented, signaling that it is part of the paragraph from the preceding page.

Words are not hyphenated at the ends of lines. This sometimes creates extra space at the end of a line, but eliminates confusion for the struggling reader.